Nitrogen

Clara MacCarald

Enslow Publishing
101 W. 23rd Street
Suite 240
New York, NY 10011
USA
enslow.com

Published in 2019 by Enslow Publishing, LLC.
101 W. 23rd Street, Suite 240, New York, NY 10011

Library of Congress Cataloging-in-Publication Data

Names: MacCarald, Clara, author.
Title: Nitrogen / Clara MacCarald.
Description: New York, NY : Enslow Publishing, LLC, 2019. | Series: Exploring the elements | Audience: Grades 5 to 8. | Includes bibliographical references and index.
Identifiers: LCCN 2017050402| ISBN 9780766099203 (library bound) | ISBN 9780766099210 (pbk.)
Subjects: LCSH: Nitrogen—Juvenile literature. | Group 15 elements—Juvenile literature. | Chemical elements—Juvenile literature.
Classification: LCC QD181.N1 M235 2019 | DDC 546/.711—dc23
LC record available at https://lccn.loc.gov/2017050402

Printed in the United States of America

To Our Readers: We have done our best to make sure all website addresses in this book were active and appropriate when we went to press. However, the author and the publisher have no control over and assume no liability for the material available on those websites or on any websites they may link to. Any comments or suggestions can be sent by email to customerservice@enslow.com.

Portions of this book appeared in *Nitrogen* by Heather Hasan.

Photo Credits: Cover, p. 1 (chemical element symbols) Jason Winter/Shutterstock.com; cover, pp. 1, 27 (liquid nitrogen) Kondor83/Shutterstock.com; p. 5 Hulton Archive/Getty Images; p. 8 Alexander A. Nedviga/Shutterstock.com; p. 10 Igor Zh./Shutterstock.com; p. 11 concept w/Shutterstock.com; p. 14 Mu Yee Ting/Shutterstock.com; p. 17 Designua/Shutterstock.com; p. 20 MicroOne/Shutterstock.com; p. 21 molekuul_be/Shutterstock.com; p. 23 NASA/Getty Images; p. 26 hiroshi teshigawara/Shutterstock.com; p. 29 bluecinema/E+/Getty Images; p. 32 BSIP/Universal Images Group/Getty Images; p. 34 Science Photo Library/Steve Gschmeissner/Brand X Pictures/Getty Images; p. 35 Universal Images Group/Getty Images; p. 38 Molekuul/Science Photo Library/Getty Images; p. 40 Tyler Olson/Shutterstock.com; p. 41 Fablok/Shutterstock.com.

Contents

Introduction

Alfred Nobel was an engineer and inventor whose most well-known invention was dynamite.

It all started when Nobel was a young man. He became interested in a nitrogen-based compound called nitroglycerine. An Italian chemist had recently invented nitroglycerine by mixing a kind of sweet syrup with acids. A colorless and oily liquid, nitroglycerine may look harmless, but it's not. The compound is one of the most powerful explosives known. A single drop can blow the head off of a hammer that strikes it!

At the time, nitroglycerine was so dangerous that no one could think of a practical purpose for it. That did not stop Nobel. He felt that nitroglycerine could be very useful for construction work or mining. He and his younger brother began experimenting with nitro-glycerine in 1859.

Over the years, they experienced several nitroglycerine explo-sions. Tragedy struck in 1864. A large explosion killed Nobel's brother and several other people. Following his brother's death, Nobel set out to find a safer way to work with this dangerous explosive.

Two years later, Nobel nearly killed himself. While working with a full test tube of nitroglycerine (enough to blow up his entire laboratory), the tube suddenly slipped out of his hand! Amazingly, the tube landed in a box filled with sawdust. The nitroglycerine spilled from the test tube and soaked into the sawdust surrounding it. Not wanting to be wasteful, Nobel used the mixture for his testing. He discovered that

Alfred Nobel, engineer and inventor. He invented dynamite.

working with nitroglycerine was much easier when it was not a liquid. This gave him an idea that would forever change the world.

Nobel began mixing nitroglycerine with other substances. Eventually, he mixed the explosive with a special kind of powdered rock. The resulting paste could be shaped into rods that would be safe to handle. Nobel had invented dynamite! Nobel went on to invent a blasting cap for his explosive. This cap allowed workers to set off the explosion at the right time. With dynamite, workers could now safely blast rock out of their way to help build tunnels, canals, and other important works.

In all, Nobel would earn 355 patents of his various inventions. Other than explosives, he created material that mimicked things like leather and silk. Nobel intended explosives like dynamite to make industry safer, but some of his discoveries became weapons of war. Perhaps out of a sense of guilt or out of a desire to promote peace, Alfred Nobel started the Nobel Peace Prize. He wanted the money he had made from his inventions to be used to make the world a safer and more peaceful place. Nobel left instructions that, following his death, his fortune was to be used to reward people for achievements in chemistry, literature, physics, and medicine, as well as for acts of peace.

1

Nitrogen Around Us

Nitrogen gas is all around you, but you wouldn't know it. You cannot see it, feel it, or even smell it. In fact, pure nitrogen does not do very much at all. For this reason, nitrogen was originally named *azote*, which is Greek for "without life." However, this name is quite ironic when you consider some of nitrogen's other qualities. Nitrogen is found in food, fertilizers, medicines, and our bodies. Without nitrogen, we would not be able to survive.

But don't let nitrogen fool you. There is also a darker side to this element. Human activity has led to nitrogen pollution that kills ocean life and threatens our health. Nitrogen is also used to make violent explosives, which can cause destruction and death. Because of its many sides, nitrogen is sometimes called the "schizophrenic element."

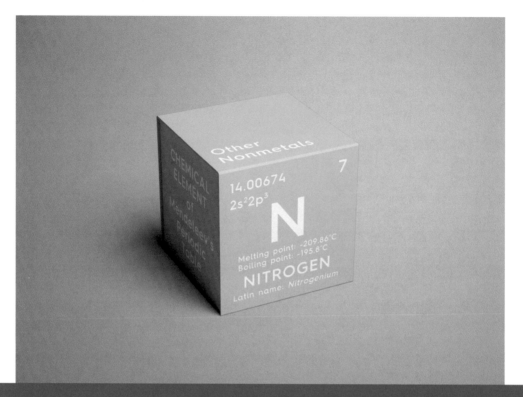

French scientist Antoine Lavoisier first suggested that this "noxious gas" was actually an element.

The Discovery of Nitrogen

Since pure nitrogen (N_2) gas does not do very much, it took a long time for people to notice it. Nitrogen was not discovered until the late eighteenth century. At that time, scientists knew air was made up of at least two gases. Many scientists were working hard to identify them.

Though several scientists were on the road to discovering nitrogen at around the same time, credit for its discovery was given to a

Scottish physicist named Daniel Rutherford. In 1772, he announced his discovery of what he called "noxious air." "Noxious" means harmful or poisonous. He named it this because animals could not breathe in it nor could candles burn when exposed to it.

However, it was not until 1775 that a French scientist named Antoine Lavoisier suggested that this "noxious gas" was actually an element. Later, Lavoisier suggested the name *azote* ("without life"), which is still what the French call nitrogen today. The term "nitrogen" was first used by Jean Antoine Chaptal in 1790. It comes from the Greek words *nitron*, which refers to a nitrogen compound used in fertilizer and gunpowder, and *genes*, meaning forming.

Scientists later realized that nitrogen is the sixth most abundant substance in the universe. It is found in the stars, in the sun, and in meteorites.

What Is Air?

In the late 1700s, scientists were only beginning to understand the air around us and what it's made of. Science has made great progress since then. Today we know the air contains several gases:

Nitrogen: 78 percent

Oxygen (O): 21 percent

Argon (Ar): 0.9 percent

Carbon Dioxide (CO_2): 0.03 percent

Hydrogen (H): 0.01 percent

Helium (He), Krypton (Kr), Neon (Ne), Xenon (Xe), Radon (Rn), and other elements and particles: 0.06%.

Now you know more than Rutherford and the other scientists of the eighteenth century did!

Nitrogen is the sixth most abundant substance in the universe. It is found in the stars, in the sun, and in meteorites.

Nitrogen is also found in Earth's atmosphere. Nitrogen (N_2) gas makes up 78 percent (four-fifths) of Earth's air. That is almost four times greater than the amount of atmospheric oxygen (O_2)!

Placing Nitrogen on the Periodic Table

Dmitry Mendeleev became the first chemist to place the elements in a large chart, called a periodic table, which he published in 1869. At the time, scientists had discovered only 62 elements. They did not yet know about atoms or that atom structure determines the behavior of elements. But they did know each element had unique properties. Mendeleev used these properties to arrange his chart. He ordered each horizontal row, or period, by atomic weight. Elements with similar characteristics were grouped into columns. For example, Mendeleev placed nitrogen in a group with phosphorus, a relationship we still recognize today.

Since Mendeleev's time, scientists have identified over 100 elements. Chemists have used new information to update and rearrange Mendeleev's tool to create the modern periodic table. The modern version lists these elements in order of increasing atomic number (number of protons in an atom's nucleus) rather than atomic weight.

PERIODIC TABLE OF THE ELEMENTS

Nitrogen is the seventh element on the periodic table of elements.

Where an element is found on the periodic table can tell you whether it is likely to be a metal, a nonmetal, or a metalloid. If you look at the periodic table, you will notice that the elements are divided by a "staircase" line. The metals are found to the left of this line, and the nonmetals are to the right. Most of the elements bordering the staircase line are metalloids, or semimetals. These elements sometimes act like metals and sometimes like nonmetals.

On the periodic table, elements are represented by one- or two-letter symbols. Nitrogen is represented by the symbol N. You can find nitrogen among the nonmetals to the right of the staircase line. A nonmetal is an element that does not have the characteristics of a metal. Metals are shiny, are flexible, and can be rolled into sheets or pulled into wires. They are also good conductors of electricity and heat. By contrast, nonmetals are not shiny. They do not conduct heat or electricity well. Nearly half of the nonmetals are colorless gases on Earth, but others occur as liquids and solids. However, unlike solid metals, solid nonmetals are brittle. They will crumble or break apart if pulled upon or hammered.

Nonmetals are often found joined with other elements in compounds. However, some elements are very important to us in their elemental, or uncombined, form. Nitrogen is one of them. Not only does nitrogen make up most of the air around us, but many industries prize nitrogen for its ability to not react with other substances. Elemental nitrogen is remarkably stable.

2

Nitrogen Atoms

///

An element cannot be broken down into different substances by ordinary means. Why not? Because each element is made up of only one kind of atom. Every atom of nitrogen is exactly the same.

Atoms are very tiny. It would take two hundred million of them, lying side by side, to form a line only a centimeter long! Amazingly, atoms are formed by even smaller particles called subatomic particles. Subatomic particles determine everything from the identity of an atom to how the atom interacts with other atoms.

Subatomic Particles

Atoms contain three types of subatomic particles: neutrons, protons, and electrons. Neutrons and protons cluster together at the center of the atom to form the nucleus. Neutrons carry no electric

Polar Light Shows

The Northern Lights (aurora borealis) and the Southern Lights (aurora australis) have fascinated people for a long time. Many cultures tell stories explaining these beautiful light shows in the sky. The Inuits of Alaska, for example, believe that they are the torches of their ancestors. What really causes these lights? The lights appear when fast-moving gusts of solar wind (a stream of electrons and protons coming from the sun) slam into the gases in Earth's atmosphere. The colors of the aurora depends on the specific gas they hit. Nitrogen molecules can produce blue, red, or purple light.

The aurora borealis as seen in Norway. There is a similar phenomenon in the Southern Hemisphere, called the aurora australis.

charge, while protons have a positive electrical charge. This gives the nucleus an overall positive electrical charge. Nitrogen has seven protons in its nucleus, so its nucleus has a charge of +7.

Around the nucleus are negatively charged electrons. The electrons are not fixed in a single position but orbit around the nucleus in layers called shells. Why do electrons remain in orbit? Because the positive nucleus attracts the negative electrons. The number of protons and electrons are usually equal, making the positive and negative charges of the atom balance each other out. Since nitrogen has seven protons, it also has seven electrons.

Elemental Differences

What makes nitrogen different from oxygen or silver? They each have a different number of protons in the nuclei of their atoms. Although most atoms have all three subatomic particles, only the proton determines the identity of an atom. Because of this, it makes sense that the periodic table organizes elements by atomic number. On the periodic table, this number shows up above the element's symbol.

Ordinary reactions cannot change an atom's nucleus, but let's imagine we could add a proton to nitrogen. Now its nucleus would go from having seven protons to having eight. Would we still have an atom of nitrogen? No. We would have an atom of oxygen (O). Just one proton makes the difference between an element that allows us to breathe and one that doesn't.

What if we take one of nitrogen's protons away? We would make carbon (C), which has six protons. Carbon is very different from nitrogen. While nitrogen is a colorless gas, we see carbon in the form of diamonds and the graphite used to make pencil lead.

Although we can't change nitrogen to oxygen in chemistry class, it really does happen—in stars! Most of the energy in stars bigger than our sun is produced by the carbon-nitrogen-oxygen cycle. The cycle begins when a carbon atom captures a hydrogen (H) atom. Hydrogen has one proton, turning carbon into nitrogen. Subsequent reactions make oxygen, carbon, and helium (He), while releasing a whole lot of energy!

Neutrons in Nitrogen

The number found below an element's symbol on the periodic table is called the atomic mass. The atomic mass is the sum of the number of protons and neutrons in the atom. Nitrogen has an atomic mass of fourteen. Knowing that the atomic mass of nitrogen is fourteen and the atomic number is seven, we can figure out how many neutrons there are in an atom of nitrogen by subtracting the two numbers:

$$14 - 7 = 7$$

Ordinary nitrogen has seven neutrons in its nucleus.

About 0.37 percent of the nitrogen in the air around us has eight neutrons per atom instead of seven. Atoms with different numbers of neutrons are called isotopes of an element. Because isotope

ISOTOPES OF NITROGEN

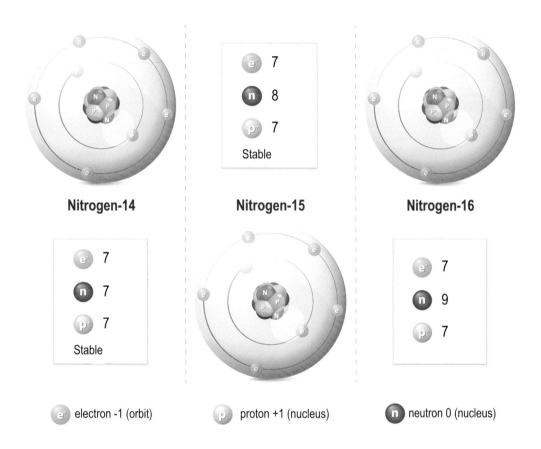

e⁻	7
n	8
p⁺	7
Stable	

Nitrogen-14

Nitrogen-15

Nitrogen-16

e⁻	7
n	7
p⁺	7
Stable	

e⁻	7
n	9
p⁺	7

e⁻ electron -1 (orbit)   p⁺ proton +1 (nucleus)   n neutron 0 (nucleus)

**Atoms with different numbers of neutrons
are called isotopes of an element.**

percentages vary in different sources of nitrogen, scientist can use
them to trace the movement of elements through natural systems.
For example, scientists can use nitrogen isotopes to determine the
source of water pollution.

The Nitrogen Family

Each vertical column of elements in the periodic table is called a group or family. Just as you might share similar characteristics with other members of your family, the elements in a group share similar properties.

Five elements make up Group VA, or the Nitrogen Family. They are nitrogen (N), phosphorus (P), arsenic (As), antimony (Sb), and bismuth (Bi). Looking down Group VA, you can see that the elements become more metallic from top to bottom. Nitrogen and phosphorus are nonmetals, arsenic and atimony are metalloids, and bismuth is a metal.

Nitrogen has two shells of electrons surrounding its nucleus. The inner shell contains two electrons, and the outer shell has five. All of the elements in Group VA have five electrons in their outermost shell. These are called valence electrons. They determine how an element behaves with other elements.

Atoms try to fill their valence shells. When they share electrons with other atoms, they create a link called a covalent bond. The bonded atoms form molecules, which make up compounds. Because all of the Group VA elements have the same number of valence electrons, they have similar chemical properties.

3

The Properties of Elemental Nitrogen

All elements have unique properties. Chemical properties of an element are characteristics that involve how that element reacts with other substances. Physical properties are characteristics that can be observed without changing the composition or identity of matter. Some examples of physical properties are color, freezing point, and phase at room temperature.

At room temperature, an element is found in one of three physical states: solid, liquid, or gas. Knowing the physical state, or phase, of an element at room temperature helps scientists to identify it.

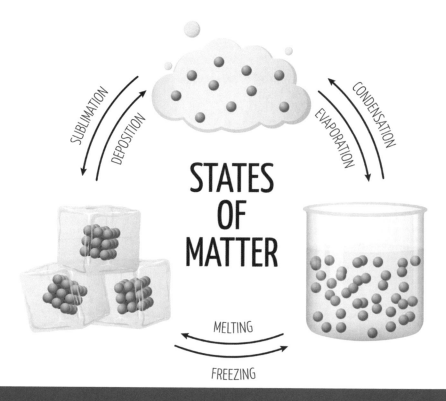

STATES OF MATTER

SUBLIMATION

DEPOSITION

CONDENSATION

EVAPORATION

MELTING

FREEZING

At room temperature, an element is found in one
of three physical states: solid, liquid, or gas.

Nitrogen differs from the rest of the elements in its family because
at room temperature nitrogen is found in the gas phase.

Two Atoms for the Price of One

Nitrogen never goes it alone. When not combined with other elements, it always forms diatomic molecules. The word "diatomic" means two atoms. A diatomic nitrogen molecule contains two nitrogen atoms and is written N_2.

Seven elements, including nitrogen, form diatomic molecules. The other six are hydrogen (H_2), oxygen (O_2), fluorine (F_2), chlorine (Cl_2), bromine (Br_2), and iodine (I_2). If you look at the periodic table, you can see that these diatomic molecules (excluding hydrogen) form the number seven! This is a good way to remember them.

Each atom shares its electrons with the other, forming a link called a covalent bond. In covalent bonds, the atoms share either one pair (two electrons), two pairs (four electrons), or three pairs (six electrons) of electrons. The more electrons that the two atoms share,

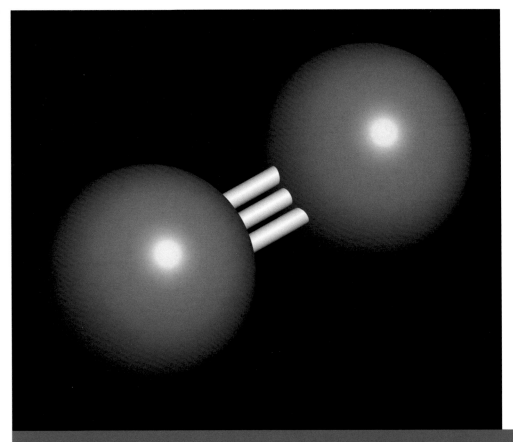

A diatomic nitrogen molecule contains two nitrogen atoms and is written as N_2. Seven elements, including nitrogen, form diatomic molecules.

the stronger their bond is. Nitrogen atoms share three pairs of electrons. This is called a triple bond and can be written like this: N≡N.

Triple bonds are very strong. The triple bond between the atoms in the N_2 molecule makes nitrogen gas very stable and unreactive. Because the nitrogen atoms are so tightly bound to each other, they do not normally react with other substances. Scientists call nitrogen, and other unreactive substances like it, inert. In order for nitrogen to react with other elements, the strong bond between the nitrogen atoms must first be broken. This takes a lot of energy!

Nitrogen in Cold Temperatures

On Earth, nitrogen is almost always a gas. However, at extremely low temperatures, nitrogen becomes a liquid or even a solid. In order for nitrogen to turn into a liquid, the temperature must be –321°F (–196°C). That's extremely cold. As a liquid, nitrogen resembles ordinary water because it is colorless and odorless. Don't drink it! If any part of you even touched liquid nitrogen, your cells would instantly freeze.

For nitrogen to reach its freezing point (the temperature at which it becomes a solid), the temperature has to drop even further, to –346°F (–210°C). The coldest temperature ever recorded on Earth was –129 °F (–89 °C). That is a long way from –346°F (–210°C).

Although the low temperatures needed to solidify nitrogen cannot be found naturally on Earth, temperatures like this can be found on another planet. Pluto is a dwarf planet far from the sun. It is so far away that the sun's warmth has trouble reaching it. During the day, the temperature on the surface of the planet reaches only a chilly –355 °F (–215 °C). If you could see Pluto, you would see that it is covered by a layer of ice made from matter that we find as gases on Earth, including nitrogen.

In 2015, the *New Horizons* spacecraft made the closest ever flyby of dwarf planet Pluto. Pluto is cold enough that nitrogen would be solid on its surface.

Nitrogen Densities

Density measures how compact an object is. That is, how much mass it contains per unit volume. Solids are denser than liquids, which in turn are denser than gases. Solid nitrogen has a density of 1.03 grams per milliliter. This is just a little higher than the density of liquid nitrogen, which is 0.81 grams per milliliter. Gaseous nitrogen has a much lower density than both solid and liquid nitrogen. Its density is only 0.00125 grams per milliliter.

Nitrogen Vehicles

When nitrogen expands from a liquid to a gas, it can make a lot of energy. Nitrogen can power an engine! Rather than giving off pollution, a nitrogen engine releases nitrogen gas. This exhaust is already found naturally in air. Some people think nitrogen will be a clean fuel for the future. In 2017, engineers in the United Kingdom tested the first bus made to run partially on nitrogen. If all goes well, someday you may see vehicles running on nitrogen along a street near you!

These densities can give you an idea about how far apart the nitrogen molecules are in each of these phases. The molecules in solid nitrogen are packed very closely together. The molecules in liquid nitrogen are not as closely packed, but, as with solid nitrogen, they still touch one another.

However, the molecules in gaseous nitrogen are quite far from one another. The molecules in the gaseous form of nitrogen are so spread out, in fact, that the volume of the gas is about 750 times greater than that of a sample of solid or liquid nitrogen of same mass. Sometimes, though, the molecules are closer together or farther apart. Unlike solids or liquids, gases do not have definite shapes or volumes. Nitrogen gas can fit in a container of almost any shape and size by either expanding or compressing. If not confined to a container, gases disperse into the atmosphere.

4

Uses of Molecular Nitrogen

Nitrogen gas is inert in most situations. This makes it endlessly useful for storing or preserving other substances. Plus, it's easy to find—vast quantities surround us. To use nitrogen, though, scientists must first separate the element from the air. Fortunately, each component of air has a unique boiling point.

First, scientists cool air until it becomes a liquid. They slowly add heat. As the boiling point of each element or compound is reached, that specific substance boils. Boiling just means it bubbles out of the liquid air as gas. Only nitrogen boils at -195.79°C (-320.42°). At that temperature, scientists collect the pure nitrogen gas for further use.

Nitrogen is also used in the oil industry to push crude oil to Earth's surface. Crude oil is a dense, dark fluid made of carbon and hydrogen.

An Inert Replacement

In contrast with nitrogen, oxygen is very reactive. It can cause other substances to rust, rot, or even explode. If normal air remained in a tank containing grain alcohol, for example, oxygen could cause the alcohol to burst into flames. Instead, people replace the air with nitrogen gas, which doesn't react with alcohol at all. Many vehicle tires are filled with nitrogen, which makes the rubber last longer than if the tires were filled with air.

Nitrogen is also used in the oil industry to push crude oil to Earth's surface. Gases other than nitrogen might react with the oil. Crude oil is a dense, dark fluid made of carbon and hydrogen. Crude oil is processed to make things like gasoline and petroleum gas, which is used for cooking and for heating houses.

Tastes Better with Nitrogen

Oxygen threatens food as well as industrial products, so food packaging often removes it. That "air" cushioning the chips inside your potato chip bag is not oxygen-rich air at all. It's nitrogen! Oxygen would cause the chips to become stale. Nitrogen does not react with them, keeping them fresh. The effect ends, however, once you

Liquid nitrogen is so cold that it allows foods to instantly reach temperatures far below freezing.

open the bag and let the nitrogen gas escape. Then it's only a matter of time until air makes your chips lose their crunch!

Food companies also value liquid nitrogen. It is so cold that it allows foods to instantly reach temperatures far below freezing. Foods like fruit and cheesecake are packaged and then sprayed with liquid nitrogen. Upon contact, the liquid absorbs heat and evaporates, leaving the food frozen. Foods treated with liquid nitrogen freeze so quickly that they do not have time to lose moisture or grow bacteria. Thawed, the food tastes fresher than if you had stuck it in your own freezer.

Some restaurants use liquid nitrogen to make food fancier. Chefs can freeze berries and break off individual sections to decorate meals. They might freeze and grind leaves to make herb dust. Even better, milk, cream, and sugar can be turned into incredibly smooth ice cream in only five minutes with liquid nitrogen. Don't try this by yourself—liquid nitrogen can damage skin and even cause explosions if handled incorrectly!

Nitrogen for Better Health

Doctors and hospitals also find the properties of nitrogen useful. Liquid nitrogen helps store blood until it is needed by patients. It can freeze viruses that will be used for vaccinations. Some medicines benefit from being packaged with gaseous nitrogen. The nitrogen keeps them from absorbing moisture or reacting with oxygen.

Sometimes, doctors take organs from one person and put them in another. They only have a few hours to work before the organs go bad. Organs can be cooled, but they can't be fully frozen. Thawing makes cracks in organ tissues. In 2017, however, researchers at the University of Minnesota were able to successfully uniformly warm cryopreserved animal heart valves and blood vessels without damage. Wasting fewer organs would mean saving more lives!

Liquid nitrogen is dangerous to handle because it causes frostbite, an injury to

Doctors and hospitals also use liquid nitrogen. Seen here, the doctors can actually boil liquid nitrogen.

body tissues resulting from exposure to very cold temperatures. However, surgeons have learned to exploit this phenomenon. Liquid nitrogen can kill unwanted or unhealthy tissue on the human body. Surgeons dab on a small amount of liquid nitrogen or use a super-chilled scalpel to scrape away the tissue. Liquid nitrogen can remove warts, tattoos, birthmarks, and skin cancer.

Frozen People

Some people believe that if they are frozen in liquid nitrogen when they die, they can be revived in the future. They believe that any diseases they may have will then be cured. This may sound strange, but there are actual facilities where people pay tens of thousands of dollars to be frozen and stored! So far no one has figured out how to bring people back from the dead, or even how to unfreeze them without damaging their bodies.

Spooky Nitrogen

If you have ever been to Disney World, you probably saw liquid nitrogen in action. Liquid nitrogen is used at theme parks, in stage plays, and in movies to create the illusion of fog or mist. At room temperature, 25°C (77°F), liquid nitrogen has the appearance of boiling water. That is because it is actually boiling as the liquid warms up! This "cold fog" is perfect for creating the creepy effect of a witch's brew or the billowy white puffs of a dragon's breath.

Bars or cafes sometimes use liquid nitrogen for smaller-scale theatrics. When liquid nitrogen is added to a drink, the cold liquid appears to steam. But customers must be careful to wait for all the nitrogen to boil off before taking a sip. You don't want frostbite anywhere, but especially not in your digestive system!

5

The Nitrogen Cycle

//

P lants and animals are full of nitrogen compounds. Without nitrogen, we couldn't exist. The nitrogen cycle describes how this essential element moves through the environment. From the air, nitrogen passes to the soil, to all living things, and then eventually back into the air.

In fact, nitrogen is responsible for much of the energy in the food chain. One of the compounds that plants use nitrogen to make is chlorophyll. Chlorophyll provides energy for photosynthesis. Nitrogen helps plants make food! Consumers such as ourselves cannot make our own food, so we must eat producers like plants to get energy.

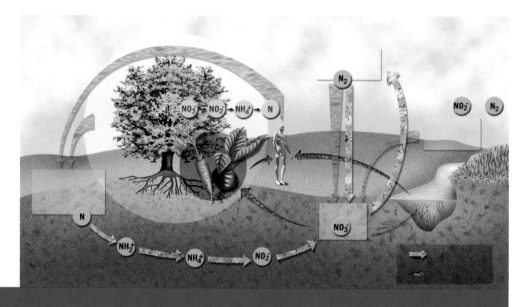

The nitrogen cycle. From the air, nitrogen passes to the soil, to all living things, and eventually back into the air.

From the Atmosphere to the Soil

Despite all the nitrogen in the atmosphere, a lack of nitrogen limits plant growth in many environments. How can that be? Most living things cannot use nitrogen gas directly. First, the molecule must be broken apart. Breaking the strong triple bond that holds the nitrogen molecule together takes a lot of energy! Most living things can't produce that kind of energy.

Nitrogen fixation is the process of converting nitrogen molecules (N_2) into nitrogen-containing compounds that plants and animals can use. Most nitrogen is fixed in one of three ways: atmospheric fixation, biological fixation, or industrial fixation.

In the atmosphere, lightning breaks a nitrogen molecule's bond using extremely high temperatures. When lightning flashes, it can heat the air as high as 33,000°C (60,000°F)! After the nitrogen molecule splits in two, the nitrogen atoms are free to react with oxygen. One atom of each element combines to form a colorless gas called nitrogen monoxide (NO).

Nitrogen monoxide then reacts with other oxygen atoms in the air to add an oxygen atom, forming nitrogen dioxide (NO_2). Nitrogen dioxide is a poisonous, reddish-brown gas with a very pungent odor. Reactions in the air and soil convert nitrogen oxides into nitrogen compounds that can be absorbed by plant roots.

Soil Bacteria

Biological fixation is the process by which most nitrogen compounds are made. Nitrogen-fixing bacteria are the only living organisms capable of using nitrogen directly from the air. Instead of using heat to break the nitrogen bonds, however, these bacteria use an enzyme. An enzyme is a molecule that speeds up a chemical reaction. You can recognize an enzyme because its name usually ends in "ase." The enzyme that bacteria use to convert nitrogen into ammonia is called nitrogenase.

Once the nitrogen bonds are broken, nitrogenase helps one atom of nitrogen bind with three atoms of hydrogen, forming ammonia (NH_3). Ammonia in the soil is easily converted into compounds that plants can use.

Some plants don't just passively absorb the nitrogen compounds. They farm their own nitrogen-fixing bacteria! Legumes such as peas create bumps on their roots that bacteria can invade. The plants take care of their guests and in return get useable nitrogen.

Nitrogen Through the Food Chain

Unlike plants, animals cannot make their own food. Animals must get nitrogen by eating plants, which have absorbed nitrogen from the soil, or from eating other animals that have fed on plants. Digestion releases the nitrogen locked in living tissues.

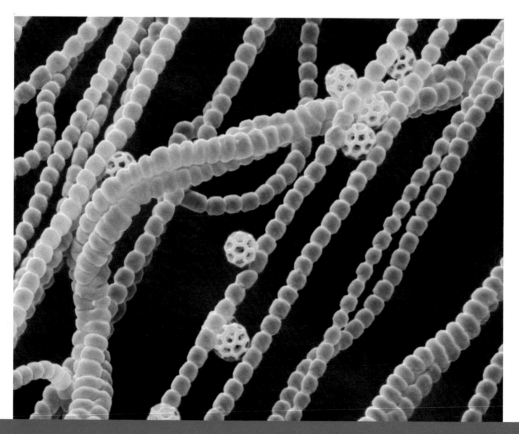

Nitrogen-fixing bacteria are the only living organisms capable of using nitrogen directly from the air.

The cycle continues when plant and animal material rots. Waste along with dead plants and animals deposit complex nitrogen compounds into the ground. Certain bacteria break these nitrogen compounds down, turning them back into ammonia. Some nitrogen from the ammonia ends up in plants, while other nitrogen is converted back into nitrogen gas, which is returned to the atmosphere. Approximately the same amount of nitrogen gas is returned to the air by these bacteria as was taken out by others. The cycle starts anew!

World-Changing Nitrogen

The majority of nitrogen compounds (60 percent) occur naturally, as in atmospheric and biological fixation. The rest is created by industrial fixation. This process, like atmospheric fixation, uses very high temperatures to break the nitrogen triple bonds. Atmospheric nitrogen (N_2) gas is combined with hydrogen gas (H_2) at temperatures of about 500°C (932°F) and pressures of about 300 atmospheres.

Industrial fixation produces ammonia, just like biological

In water, excess nitrogen can lead to algal blooms, which are out-of-control populations of bacteria.

fixation. Ammonia can be used to make plant fertilizer. Industrial fixation has revolutionized modern agriculture. Nitrogen-based fertilizers have increased the productivity of farm fields and helped to feed the more than seven billion people living on Earth. Unfortunately, only about half of the fertilizer added to the ground ends up in crops. Some washes into streams, rivers, and ultimately the ocean.

More of a good thing isn't always better. In water, excess nitrogen can lead to algal blooms, which are out-of-control populations of bacteria. Algal blooms create huge problems. Sometimes, the bacteria produce toxins. They can use up the oxygen in water, killing other living things. Agricultural runoff creates huge dead zones in both oceans and fresh water. Every spring, a dead zone about the size of New Jersey develops in the Gulf of Mexico at the mouth of the Mississippi River. Algal blooms are a growing problem all over the world.

Self-Fertilizing Plants

The success of modern agriculture relies on fertilizers, but fertilizers are expensive and polluting. Developing other ways to feed plants could help both poor farmers and the environment. Although many plants host nitrogen-fixing bacteria, no plant can use atmospheric nitrogen by itself—so far. Some scientists in Australia are looking to change that. They are trying to introduce the gene that makes nitrogenase to cereal crops. Someday, crops like wheat and corn could fix nitrogen from the atmosphere all by themselves!

6

Nitrogen Compounds and Where to Find Them

Nitrogen is everywhere. It's in the air, in our bodies, and in many useful compounds. Nitrogen compounds form our bodies, make our body systems work, and pass on our traits to the next generation. They can make a dentist visit more pleasant, or they can help catch a criminal. They can even threaten your life—or save it! Here is a few of the many molecules that contain this adaptable element.

Nitrogen Compounds in Your Body

Make a fist. Breath in. Blink your eyes. Everything you do requires protein, a nitrogen compound. During digestion, the protein in food is broken down into amino acids. Your body uses the twenty common types of amino acids as building blocks to make thousands of different proteins.

Protein is found in your hair, your skin, and your organs. Proteins are an essential part of your muscles and your skeleton. Without protein, you'd fall in a heap! Some proteins are enzymes, like nitrogenase from the last chapter. There are many kinds of enzymes in your body and each serves a specific purpose. Without enzymes, many reactions in the body would be too slow to support life.

How does your body know how to arrange amino acids into specific proteins? That is the work of another nitrogen compound called DNA. We inherit DNA from our parents. When people talk about genes, they are really talking about this compound. DNA tells the body how to build itself

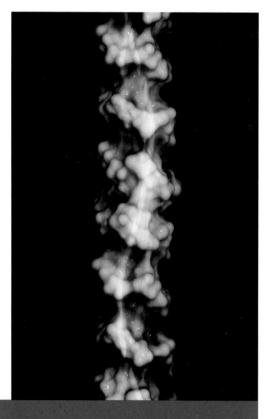

Protein is found in your hair, your skin, and your organs. Proteins are an essential part of your muscles and your skeleton.

and how to function. Stretches of the DNA molecule contain codes that specify the order in which the amino acids should be linked. These recipes are used to make all of the different kinds of proteins found in your body, from muscles to enzymes.

Dentists and Detectives

Laughing gas is the common name for nitrous oxide (N_2O). This colorless, sweet-smelling gas got its name from the way that people act when they inhale it. People laugh or cry uncontrollably. Although the compound sounds silly, it can be dangerous. If people inhale large amounts of laughing gas, they won't get enough oxygen and can die.

Small amounts of laughing gas can relieve pain. Dentists have been using this gas to make their patients more comfortable since the 1840s. Even today, if you go to the dentist to have a tooth removed, he or she might give you a mask so you can breathe in a mixture of this compound and oxygen.

DNA Fingerprinting

Except for identical twins, everyone has a unique set of genes. Sometimes, people leave bits of DNA behind during a crime. Labs can try to match DNA found at the scene to a suspect. Unfortunately, the lab needs to have a sample from the guilty party. Some researchers are learning to read DNA code. They can use an unknown sample of genetic material to predict that the person who left it behind had blue eyes and yellow hair, for example. Along with other evidence, these predictions can help catch a crook!

People tend to laugh or cry when they inhale nitrous oxide, but small amounts relieve pain and make certain medical procedures possible.

Silver nitrate ($AgNO_3$) has an important power—it can catch criminals! Each person has a unique pattern of ridges found on their fingertips. When you touch a surface, the oil on your skin leaves behind this pattern. Fingerprints are usually invisible. But detectives can find them by spraying them with silver nitrate. The print turns a brownish color. The print can then be photographed and used to find a criminal.

Dirty Air

The heat from your car's hot engine forms nitrogen monoxide, just like lightning does. Power stations, schools, homes, and offices also produce nitrogen monoxide. When this poisonous gas reacts with oxygen, it forms nitrogen dioxide. This brown, foul-smelling gas is one of the main components of smog, the brown haze you see hanging over some city areas. Nitrogen dioxide dissolves in rainwater and forms nitric acid, one of the ingredients in acid rain. Acid rain kills fish and vegetation and eats away at buildings and statues.

One of the first explosives ever used was gunpowder, or potassium nitrate. This nitrogen compound was invented over 1,000 years ago!

Fireplaces, gas stoves, and water heaters also produce nitrogen dioxide indoors. Nitrogen dioxide can irritate your eyes, nose, and throat. It can also make it easier for you to get lung infections. You can keep this gas from building up in your house by opening windows and vents.

The Dangers of Nitrogen

One of the first explosives ever used was gunpowder, or potassium nitrate. This nitrogen compound was invented over 1,000 years ago! Today, two common nitrogen compounds are trinitrotoluene (TNT) and nitroglycerine. TNT is the explosive used in bombs, and nitroglycerine is the explosive part of dynamite.

Why are some nitrogen compounds so explosive? Because they are extremely unstable. The nitrogen atoms in them are eager to reform diatomic nitrogen (N_2) molecules. Remember all of that energy that had to be added to the nitrogen molecules to get them to form compounds? That same amount of energy is released when a tiny spark, a flame, or heat triggers the compound to break apart. Nitrogen (N_2) gas reforms. The nitrogen gas expands very quickly, and this makes for a pretty big explosion!

Air bags exploit a dangerous nitrogen compound, sodium azide, to quickly cushion you in a car accident. When sensors detect a crash, they trigger a small explosion. The heat produced causes sodium azide to break apart. Nitrogen gas fills the air bag. According to the National Highway Traffic Safety Administration, air bags saved 39,976 lives from 1987 to 2012.

It's simply another example of how nitrogen is the two-sided element. Now you know that nitrogen can be both incredibly stable and explosively destructive. Without the nitrogen cycle, living things couldn't exist. Whether nitrogen is the air around us or cycling through the food chain, keeping our food fresh or blasting through rock, it's a good thing there's nitrogen!

Glossary

amino acids Building blocks that make up proteins.

atomic number The number of protons in the nucleus of an atom.

atomic weight The mass of one atom of an element.

diatomic Having to do with two atoms forming a molecule.

DNA Genetic material in the body that codes for proteins.

electron A negatively charged particle found in shells outside the nucleus of an atom.

element The basic matter that all things are made of, or any matter made up of one kind of atom.

enzyme A molecule in living things that speeds up a chemical reaction.

inert Not reacting chemically with other substances.

isotope An atom of an element with a different number of neutrons.

molecule The smallest bit of matter before it gets broken down into its basic parts, or atoms.

neutron A particle within the nucleus of an atom that contains no charge.

nucleus The positively charged central portion of an atom.

photosynthesis The process by which plants and some other organisms use sunlight to form food from carbon dioxide and water.

proton A positively charged particle within the nucleus of an atom.

valence Having to do with the outer shell of an atom.

Further Reading

Books

Bortz, Fred. *The Periodic Table of the Elements and Dmitry Mendeleyev.* New York, NY: Rosen Publishing, 2014.

Dakers, Diane. *The Nitrogen Cycle.* St. Catharines, ON: Crabtree Publishing, 2015.

Jackson, Tom. *The Elements Book: A Visual Encyclopedia of the Periodic Table.* New York, NY: DK Publishing, 2017.

Websites

Elements for Kids

www.ducksters.com/science/chemistry/nitrogen.php
Explore the properties of nitrogen!

Science for Kids

www.scienceforkidsclub.com/nitrogen.html
Some facts about nitrogen along with a recipe for using liquid nitrogen to make ice cream!

Steve Spangler Science

www.stevespanglerscience.com/lab/experiments/ liquid-nitrogen-cloud-of-fun/
Observe Steve Spangler use liquid nitrogen to make spooky clouds move—and a nitrogen explosion!

Bibliography

Allen, Robert S., Kimberley Tilbrook, Andrew C. Warden, Peter C. Campbell, Vivien Rolland, Surinder P. Singh, and Craig C. Wood. "Expression of 16 Nitrogenase Proteins Within the Plant Mitochondrial Matrix." *Frontiers in Plant Science* 8(2017):287. https://www.ncbi.nlm.nih.gov/pmc /articles/PMC5334340/.

Ebbing, Darrell D. *General Chemistry*. Fourth ed. Boston, MA: Houghton Mifflin Company, 1993.

Gibbs, Wayt, and Nathan Myhrvold. "Cryogenic Cooking." *Scientific American*, August 1, 2011. https://www.scientificamerican.com /article/cryogenic-cooking/.

McMurry, John. E., and Robert C. Fay. *General Chemistry, Atoms First*. Upper Saddle River, NJ: Pearson Prentice Hall, 2010.

Merola, Joseph S. "How Do Air Bags Work?" *Scientific American*. 2017. https://www.scientificamerican.com/article/how-do-air-bags-work/.

"Nanowarming for Regenerative Medicine: Improving Tissue Cryopreservation by Inductive Heating of Magnetic Nanoparticles," *Science Translational Medicine* 01 Mar 2017: Vol. 9, Issue 379, eaah4586 DOI: 10.1126/scitranslmed.aah4586. http://stm .sciencemag.org/content/9/379/eaah4586.

National Aeronautics and Space Administration. "Pluto: The Ice Plot Thickens." July 15, 2015. https://www.nasa.gov/image-feature /pluto-the-ice-plot-thickens.

National Highway Traffic Safety Administration. "Air Bags." https://www
    .nhtsa.gov/equipment/air-bags.

Nobelprize.org. "Alfred Nobel—His Life and Work." 2017. https://www
    .nobelprize.org/alfred_nobel/biographical/articles/life-work/.

Parsons, Paul, and Gail Dixon. *The Periodic Table: A Visual Guide to the
    Elements*. New York, NY: Quercus Editions, 2013.

Stwertka, Albert. *A Guide to the Elements*. Second ed. New York, NY:
    Oxford University Press, 2002.

Swinburne University of Technology. "CNO Cycle." Cosmos. http://
    astronomy.swin.edu.au/cosmos/C/CNO+cycle.

University of Minnesota. "Groundbreaking Technology Successfully
    Rewarms Large-Scale Tissues Preserved at Low Temperatures
    [Press Release]." March 1, 2017. https://www.eurekalert.org/pub_
    releases/2017-03/uom-gts022717.php.

US Environmental Protection Agency. "Nutrient Pollution: The Problem."
    March 10, 2017. https://www.epa.gov/nutrientpollution/problem.

US Geological Survey. "Resources on Isotopes: Periodic Table—Nitrogen."
    Last updated January 2004. https://wwwrcamnl.wr.usgs.gov/isoig
    /period/n_iig.html.

"World's First Liquid Nitrogen Hybrid Bus Completes Trials." Mira. May 31,
    2017. https://www.horiba-mira.com/news-and-events/2017/may
    /first-liquid-nitrogen-hybrid-bus-completes-trials.

Index